Story Link® Program

SPACE JAM™

Adapted by James Preller
Based on the screenplay written by
Leo Benvenuti & Steve Rudnick and Timothy Harris & Herschel Weingrod

© 1996 Warner Bros.

SCHOLASTIC INC.
New York Toronto London Auckland Sydney

ISBN 0-590-94554-8

SJSC17

Copyright © 1996 by Warner Bros. All rights reserved. SPACE JAM, characters, names and all related indicia are trademarks of Warner Bros. © 1996.

12 11 10 9 8 7 6 5 4 3 2   6 7 8 9/9 0 1/0

Designed by Joan Ferrigno

Printed in the U.S.A.   23

First Scholastic printing, November 1996

Have you ever gazed into the night sky, stared at the glittering distant stars, and wondered if there was intelligent life in outer space?

Well . . . FORGET ABOUT IT!

Life, sure. Intelligent? You decide. . . .

At an intergalactic theme park called Moron Mountain, business had fallen on hard times. And the owner — a big bully named Swackhammer — was furious.

"We need new attractions!" Swackhammer screamed. His pint-size helpers — the wimpy Nerdlucks — feverishly nodded in agreement.

Swackhammer roared, "We need something . . . nutty. We need something . . . wacky. We need something . . . something . . . something . . . "

"Looney?" Bupkus offered.

"Looney!" Swackhammer gleefully shouted. "That's the word I was looking for — looney! Get the Looney Tunes! Bring 'em here!"

Meanwhile, back in Looney Tune Land, Bugs Bunny had problems of his own.

"All wight, you pesky wabbit," said Elmer Fudd as he aimed his shotgun. "I've got you now!"

Suddenly a spaceship landed right on top of Elmer! Our fluffy-tailed hero was saved. Well, almost.

The five Nerdlucks — Bang, Bupkus, Blanko, Pound, and Nawt — stepped off the spaceship. "We seek the one they call Bugs Bunny," Pound said.

Bugs scratched his chin, amused. "Hmmm, Bugs Bunny. Does he have great big long ears, like this?"

"Yeah," the Nerdlucks answered.

"Does he say, 'What's up, Doc?' like this: 'Eh, what's up, Doc?' "

"YEAH!" the aliens responded, their excitement growing.

"Nope, never heard of him." Bugs giggled and started to walk away.

ZAPPP! Bugs turned to see five smoking ray guns pointed right at his kisser. "Okay, bunny," Pound demanded. "Gather up your Tune pals. We're taking you for a ride."

In the ordinary world of humans, basketball superstar
Michael Jordan could only *wish* he had gotten a ride from
five freaky aliens. Instead, he was in a car with someone far
stranger — Stan Podolak, the assistant for Michael's baseball
team, the Birmingham Barons. Though Stan meant well, he
often tried a little *too* hard.

"Thanks for the ride," Michael said, relieved to escape Stan's beat-up jalopy of a car.

Stan gazed out the car window. "This is a nice house. If you need anything done around it, I'll be more than happy to help you . . . a little painting — "

"No. I'm fine, thanks," Michael interrupted.

Stan tried again, "Anything you need."

"You gave me a ride," Michael said. "I appreciate it. Thanks."

Michael was happy to be home with his family. It had been a bad day on the baseball field. He said hello to his three children — Jeffrey, Marcus, and Jasmine. He kissed Juanita, his lovely wife.

In the living room, the kids were watching television. Michael entered to hear a reporter say, "Let's face it. Michael Jordan's baseball experiment is just not working. Today he went oh-for-four with three strikeouts."

"Is this the only thing on TV?" Michael asked, irritated.

Michael picked up the remote and channel surfed until he found something good. Something fun. Something . . . looney. It was the Road Runner and Wile E. Coyote.

"There you go," Michael said.

On television, Wile E. Coyote watched for signs of his speedy rival, the Road Runner. Suddenly, Porky Pig appeared in the middle of the road.

"Stop this cartoon!" pleaded the panicked pig. "We got an emergency Cartoon Character Local 96 union meeting!"

"*Beep-beep.*" Road Runner, Porky, and Wile E. Coyote rushed off.

In the Jordan living room, Marcus stared at the empty screen. "Where did they go?"

Chaos ruled Looney Tune Town Hall. All the famous Looney
Tune characters were there — Sylvester, Taz, Daffy Duck, Foghorn
Leghorn, and more. Bugs and Elmer appeared on the stage, wrapped
in heavy chains. Bugs informed the gathered crowd, "These little
guys would like to make an announcement."

Pound stepped up to the microphone. "You are now our prisoners!"

Nawt sweetly explained, "We are taking you to our theme park in outer space, where you will be our slaves."

The Looney Tunes couldn't believe it. They erupted in laughter. But when the Nerdlucks pulled out their roasty-toasty ray guns, it wasn't funny anymore. Thinking quickly, Bugs scribbled some rules in a book. "You gotta give us a chance to defend ourselves," he said, pointing to a page.

The Nerdlucks reluctantly agreed. After all, a rule was a rule.

In a small conference room, Bugs talked it over with the Looney Tunes. "Okay, let's analyze the competition. We've got a small race of invading aliens."

"Small arms. Short legs," said Daffy.

"Not vewy fast," Elmer added.

"Tiny little guys," Sylvester observed.

Hmmmm. Bugs clapped his hands in triumph.

He walked up to the Nerdlucks and announced, "We challenge you to a basketball game!"

The Nerdlucks didn't know *anything* about basketball! Of course, they could learn. They could shoot and dribble and practice day and night.

They *could.* But then they saw how hard the game was. And they decided it would be much easier to cheat!

Using a mysterious purple vapor, the Nerdlucks went to professional basketball games and stole the talent from some of the greatest players on the planet: Patrick Ewing, Charles Barkley, Shawn Bradley, Muggsy Bogues, and Larry Johnson! Suddenly, these five basketball stars couldn't run, shoot, or jump.

The next day on television, an announcer reported, "In a shocking development, five players have been placed on the disabled list in the last twenty-four hours, all suffering from the same mysterious ailment."

This could only mean trouble for the Looney Tunes. . . .

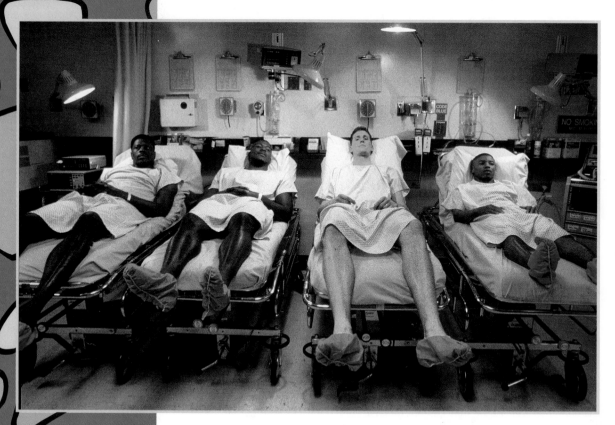

At the first practice, Bugs took a good, hard look at his teammates. It was not a pretty sight. Bugs asked, "Now, which of you maroons has ever played basketball before?"

And the answer was . . . *nobody!*

Next it was the aliens' turn to practice. As they warmed up, the little Nerdlucks looked ridiculous. Daffy sneered, "Too bad you can't practice getting taller, boys!"

But hold on to your gym shorts. Each of the aliens drank a vial of purple liquid. Then they put their tiny hands on a basketball. Suddenly the tiny aliens weren't tiny anymore. They were big. They were huge. Or, as Sylvester said, "Sufferin' succotash! *They're Monstars!*"

A worried Bugs Bunny decided, "I think we might need a little bit of help."

Far from Looney Tune Land, Michael Jordan, his pals, and Stan Podolak were enjoying a relaxing day on the golf course. A routine, humdrum, run-of-the-mill day. But not for long.

Michael reached for his ball in the cup. "Uh-oh." He got sucked down into the hole!

Bewildered, Michael slowly looked around. He couldn't believe his eyes. Michael saw Bugs, Tweety, Porky, Daffy, Elmer, and the rest of the Looney Tunes. "What's going on here?" Michael asked.

Bugs jumped into Michael's lap. "You see, these aliens came from outer space and they want to make us slaves in their theme park. They're little, so we challenged them to a basketball game. But then they show up and they ain't so little. . . . What I'm trying to say is . . . WE NEED YOUR HELP!"

Michael soon realized he was with a wild and crazy cast of characters. "You guys are nuts!" he said.

Porky shook his head. "C-c-correction: We are Looney Tunes!"

CRASH! Suddenly the rude and crude Monstars strutted into the room . . . right through the wall.

"We're the Mean Team," Pound said menacingly.

The Monstars laughed at Michael. They called him chump.
They called him chicken. They even called him . . . *baldy*. But
Michael didn't get mad. Not until one of the Monstars swatted
Tweety.

Michael helped Tweety up. He looked into the pleading eyes
of Bugs, Daffy, and Yosemite. Cartoons or not, these guys *needed*
help. Michael had seen enough. "Let's play some basketball."

Before he could play hoops, Michael needed sneakers and shorts. So Bugs and Daffy went to fetch Michael's gym bag from his house. But on the way back they were followed by Stan Podolak!

Down in Looney Tune Land, it looked as if Michael Jordan still had his old basketball skills. He could spin, leap, soar, and jam. He was a double-pumping, pure-shooting, tongue-wagging superstar. In a word, Michael was amazing.

Stan cautiously peered into the room. He was shocked to find a basketball court — filled with cartoon characters — and Michael Jordan!

Stan rushed up to Michael and hugged him. "Thank goodness you're all right," he cried.

"C'mon, Stan," Michael said, "don't hug me."

Finally, it was the night of the ultimate game. The stadium announcer roared, "Ladies and gentlemen, the starting lineup for the Tune Squad!"

One by one, the players were introduced: the Tasmanian Devil, Lola Bunny, Daffy Duck, Bugs Bunny, and Michael Jordan! Everyone was pumped and confident — until the challengers arrived. The Monstars looked mean, nasty, brutal, and not very nice.

During the first half, the Monstars pummeled the Tune Squad. They ran over players. They stole the ball, slammed monster jams, and injured perfectly harmless cartoon characters. The only bright spot for the Tune Squad was the outstanding play of Michael Jordan. But despite Michael's high-flying heroics, the first half ended with the score: Monstars 64, Tune Squad 18.

Things looked bleak in the Tune Squad locker room. The Tunes felt banged up and defeated. Michael tried to rally the team. "Come on," he urged. "We can still win this game. We gotta believe in ourselves!"

A door opened and a wobbly Stan entered the room. He looked like a mess. Daffy observed, "Looks like Stan just had a close encounter with a bug zapper!"

Stan explained what happened: "Monstars!"

The Tune Squad
needed help . . . fast.
When no one was
looking, Bugs grabbed
Michael's water bottle
and wrote, MICHAEL'S
SECRET STUFF. Though
the bottle was filled
with ordinary water,
all the Looney Tunes
thought it contained
some kind of magical
formula. They
eagerly swigged
it down. Now
they believed
in themselves!

The Tune Squad came out of the locker room like a new team. Bugs, Lola, and the Tasmanian Devil all made spectacular plays. And Michael did it all — rebounded, blocked shots, stole the ball, and scored. Everybody on the team contributed. Even Stan made a basket!

With just ten seconds left, the Monstars led, 89–88. Michael called time-out. He said, "Somebody steal the ball, get it to me, and I'll score before the time runs out."

In a blinding flash, Road Runner stole the ball. Suddenly, Michael had it.

But the Monstars weren't about to let him shoot. They raised their arms to block the ball. They guarded him. They even growled at him. Yet nothing could stop his Royal Highness. Still holding the ball, Michael jumped and stretched — up and up, higher and higher, farther and farther — JORDAN SCORES!

The Tune Squad wins it! Tune Squad 90, Monstars 89.

Swackhammer was furious. But the Monstars were bigger than he was. They weren't afraid of him anymore. So they sent him on a long trip into space.

Michael forced the Monstars to give him the players' talent. Then he raced to the human world. "You want your games back?" he asked the players. "Just touch the ball." Now they would be stars once more.

As for Michael Jordan? Well, he's back where he belongs — flying high above the rim, a basketball in his hand, looking to score.